SUPERHERO SCHOOL

The Revenge of the Green Meanie

Also by Alan MacDonald

The Troll Trouble series:
Trolls Go Home!
Trolls United
Trolls On Hols
Goat Pie

The History of Warts series:
Custardly Wart: Pirate (third class)
Ditherus Wart: (accidental) Gladiator
Honesty Wart: Witch Hunter!
Sir Bigwart: Knight of the Wonky Table

The Iggy the Urk series:
Oi, Caveboy!
Arrrrgh! Slimosaur!
Euuugh! Eyeball Stew!
BOOOM!

SUPERHERO SCHOOL

The Revenge of the Green Meanie

Alan MacDonald

BLOOMSBURY

LONDON NEW DELHI NEW YORK SYDNEY

Bloomsbury Publishing, London, New Delhi, New York and Sydney

First published in Great Britain in May 2014 by Bloomsbury Publishing Plc
50 Bedford Square, London WC1B 3DP

www.bloomsbury.com

A CIP catalogue record for this book is available from the British Library

ISBN 978 1 4088 2523 5

Printed and bound in Great Britain by CPI Group (UK) Ltd, Croydon CRO 4YY

1 3 5 7 9 10 8 6 4 2

Chapter 1
Dangerboy

Dangerboy's cape whipped around him. The city spread out below like a rumpled red duvet.

Mrs Button poked her head round the door. 'How many times? No jumping on the bed!'

'But Dangerboy has to save mankind from Dr Doom!' said Stan.

'Well, tell Dangerboy his dinner's getting cold.'

Stan sighed. By now Dr Doom would be halfway to his secret volcano lair. Stan peeled off his superhero mask and hung it on the bedpost. He'd have to finish saving the world after dinner.

Halfway downstairs he stopped and scratched

his left ear. It was tingling, which probably meant
sprouts for supper.

'Come on, lad, we're hungry,' said Mr
Button, looking up.

'I had to practise my surprise attack move,'
said Stan. 'Dr Doom was getting away . . .'

'Well, if he's a doctor, he's probably very
busy,' said Mrs Button.

Stan sat down and looked at his plate. His tingling ear never failed.

Mr Button speared a chip on his fork. 'Have you given any thought to what you might like to be if you don't become an – um – superhero?'

'I'll be a superhero,' said Stan without hesitation.

'Yes, but it's good to have other options,' said Mrs Button.

'And it's good to have ambition,' Mr Button sighed. 'But not everyone can be a superhero. Do you actually know any superheroes?'

'What about Captain Courageous?' said Stan.

Every week the *Gormley Gazette* reported on Captain Courageous's latest daring adventures. Stan had pictures and posters of him all over his walls. Beside his bed was a plastic model of the superhero that he'd got free in a packet of cornflakes.

'Exactly,' said Mr Button.

'What do you mean?' asked Stan.

'Well, he can fly and he's got superpowers. It's difficult to learn things like that.'

'Maybe he started off by jumping on the bed too,' said Stan. 'Then one day he discovered he could fly. That's why I need to practise.'

'What for?'

'So that I'm ready,' said Stan, smearing a chip with ketchup. 'You don't know – I could get a call at any time.'

A letter came through the door and landed on the doormat.

Mrs Button went into the hall and returned holding a long silver envelope with no postmark or stamp, just a name and address.

'Ooh, it's for you, Stan!' she cried.

'Me?' Stan looked up. He never got

letters – except when he had an overdue library book. But this didn't look as if it came from the library; it looked exciting.

Well open it then

Stan tore the envelope open. Inside was a letter written in purple ink. It was short . . . and baffling.

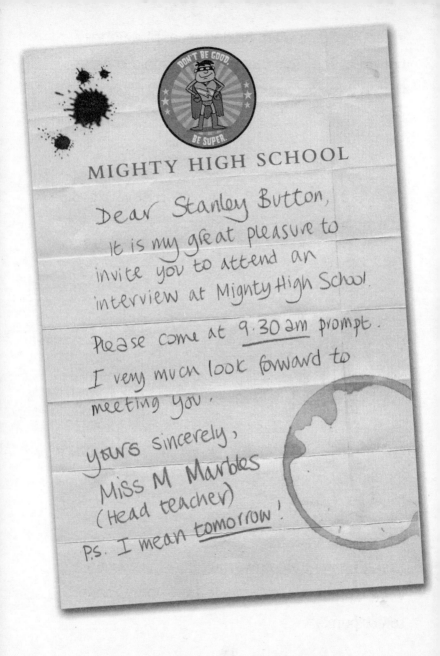

There was a stunned silence. Mrs Button looked at Stan. Mr Button set down his knife and fork. 'I've never heard of a school called Mighty High.'

'Well, isn't this exciting?' said his mum.

'But what's it for?' asked Mr Button. 'You go to school already. What's this Mighty High?'

'I think it's that new place they've opened in that abandoned building,' said Mrs Button. 'It might be one of these schools that hands out thingummybobs – you know . . .'

'PlayStations?' said Stan hopefully.

'No, scholarships – scholarships for clever children,' said his mum. 'Perhaps your teacher got in touch.'

Stan couldn't imagine why Mr Horrocks would recommend him. Had they sent the letter to the wrong person? But there was his name, written on the envelope in black and white – or rather purple.

Mr Button pushed his plate away. 'I don't know. It's a bit odd,' he said, shaking his head. 'Schools don't usually send invitations out of the blue. And what kind of name is Mighty High?'

Stan looked at the letter again. 'Can't I go to the interview?' he said. 'Just to find out what they want.'

He wondered why they had written to him. Had they been watching him in secret? Did they know things about him? Like the fact that he had a secret identity: Dangerboy, super-crime-fighter, righter of wrongs and wronger of rights.

Mrs Button cleared away the plates. 'Oh, let the boy go, Derek.'

'Please, Dad!' Stan begged.

Mr Button sighed. 'Well, I suppose there's no harm in going along.'

Stan cheered.

His mum smiled and nodded. 'You'll need a clean shirt,' she said. 'And don't go wearing that mask – we don't want them thinking you're peculiar.'

Chapter 2
Mighty High

The following morning, Stan found himself sitting in a dusty, cluttered, high-ceilinged room. On the wall was a sign which bore the motto:

A desk was occupied by a marmalade cat purring loudly. Behind it sat a woman with wild, frizzy grey hair.

'So, you wanted to see me?' said Miss Marbles.

Mrs Button looked confused. 'Actually, I thought *you* wanted to see *us*,' she said.

'Did I? What for?' Miss Marbles frowned.

'You sent a letter to my son Stan. I've got it here,' said Mrs Button, producing the envelope from her handbag.

Miss Marbles put on her glasses and studied the contents of the letter.

'Ah yes.' She nodded. 'I recognise my writing. We send out these letters from time to time to promising students.'

'Oh,' said Mrs Button, pleased. 'Is Stan a promising student?'

'That's what we're here to find out,' said Miss Marbles. 'What do you think, Stan? Are you promising?'

'I'm not sure,' mumbled Stan. 'Mr Horrocks says I never listen.'

Miss Marbles tutted. 'And is Mr Horrocks worth listening to?'

Stan pulled a face. 'Not really – he goes on a bit.'

'Then that's entirely his fault,' said the head teacher. She got to her feet, scooping up the marmalade cat, which struggled in vain to escape. Miss Marbles stroked its head till it rolled on its back and went back to purring.

'Now,' she said, 'I'd like to ask you a few questions. Don't worry – there are no right or wrong answers. Just say what you think.'

'OK.' Stan nodded, shifting in his seat. It sounded like a test. If it was maths or spelling, he was in big trouble. His mum patted his arm encouragingly.

Miss Marbles took a crumpled sheet of paper from a drawer and began. 'So, have you ever woken up on the roof of a tall building?' she asked.

Stan blinked at her, a little startled.

'Yes or no?' said Miss Marbles.

'Umm, no, I don't think so,' said Stan.

The head teacher nodded. 'Have you ever lifted something heavy – a car, for instance?'

'No,' said Stan.

'What about a lorry or a bus?'

'No,' said Stan again. 'I've been *on* a bus, if that counts.'

'Hmm,' said Miss Marbles. She stroked the

cat's soft belly and reeled off questions so quickly that Stan could hardly keep up.

'Have you ever felt you might burst into flames?'

'Ever melted anything with your eyes?'

'Not really.'

'Do you hear things?'

'What sort of things?'

'You know, *things*: voices, messages, talking animals?'

'Er, no,' said Stan.

'Have you ever fallen upstairs?'

'Don't you mean downstairs?' asked Stan.

'Not at all,' said Miss Marbles. 'Any fool can fall downstairs; falling upstairs is harder.'

'Then I haven't,' said Stan. He was starting to think he might have scored better on a spelling test.

Miss Marbles went back to her desk and shuffled through a pile of papers till she found a card. She gave it to Stan. 'Take a look at these pictures,' she said. 'Do you recognise them?'

'Yes,' Stan nodded.

'And have you got any of them?'

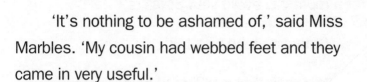

'NO!' said Stan.

'It's nothing to be ashamed of,' said Miss Marbles. 'My cousin had webbed feet and they came in very useful.'

Stan glanced at his mum, who clearly thought Miss Marbles was as nutty as a fruitcake.

The head teacher sat back down and wrote something in a notebook. The ginger cat had escaped under the desk. 'Well, I think that will do for now.' She sighed. 'As far as I can tell, you are perfectly normal.'

'Thank goodness for that!' laughed Mrs Button.

'Yes, there are many schools where normal children do very well,' said Miss Marbles. 'Unfortunately Mighty High isn't one of them. Our children are – how shall I put it – *extra*-ordinary.'

Stan wondered if extraordinary meant they had superpowers. It would certainly explain some of the potty questions. Miss Marbles was still talking. 'Let's do a few physical checks. Stand up for a moment, would you, Stan?'

Stan did as he was told.

'You see that wall?' said Miss Marbles, pointing to the far end of the room. 'I'd like you to run at it.'

'Sorry?' said Stan.

'Run at it as fast as you can. Don't worry about the damage.'

'But . . . it's a wall,' Stan pointed out.

'I know, but let's just see what happens.'

Stan looked at his mum, who widened her eyes. There was nothing for it. He took a few deep breaths and ran at the wall. Maybe it hid some sort of secret doorway that would reveal itself at the last moment?

'There, that wasn't so difficult, was it?' asked the head teacher, peering down at him. 'Are you OK?'

'I think so.' Stan sat up, rubbing his head. 'Did I do it right?'

'Perfectly well, though some children make more of a dent,' said Miss Marbles.

Stan felt that in some vague way he had failed the test.

'Well, I think that's all, unless you have any questions,' said Miss Marbles.

Mrs Button blinked. She had a million and one questions but she hardly knew where to start. Miss Marbles hadn't said a word about things like class sizes, lessons or homework.

'Er, what about school dinners?' she asked at random.

'Eat them, by all means,' said Miss Marbles. 'Though I wouldn't advise it. Mrs Sponge is the most terrible cook.'

'And school uniform?' asked Mrs Button.

'We don't have one,' said Miss Marbles. 'Of course, I insist on capes, but they mustn't get under their feet.'

'Capes?' asked Mrs Button faintly.

'Yes. Children like to choose their own

colour – red, gold, silver, it's quite up to you. Now if that's everything, I really must get on. May I show you out?'

Stan followed the head along the corridor. Again he had the sinking feeling that he had failed without knowing why. It was like playing a game where no one told you the rules. And now that the interview was over, he felt strangely disappointed. Why wasn't he extraordinary like the children who got into the school?

They stepped outside into the bright morning light. Suddenly Stan's ears began to prickle. It was the strange feeling he always got when something bad or alarming was about to happen. He didn't stop to think.

'LOOK OUT!' he cried, shoving Miss Marbles
out of the way.

'Good gracious! Where did that come from?' Miss Marbles said. They all looked up. The flowerpot must have somehow slipped from a row of pots above the entrance. Stan found Miss Marbles was looking at him with new interest.

'How did you know it was going to fall?' she asked.

Stan shrugged. 'I don't know. I just knew.'

The head took off her glasses and wiped them clean. 'Astonishing!' she cried. 'Has this happened before?'

'All the time,' said Mrs Button. 'It's like living with a human alarm clock. You never know when he's going to go off.'

'ESP,' said Miss Marbles. 'Extrasensory Perception. It means that Stan senses things. He feels them even before they happen.'

'I don't know about that,' said Mrs Button. 'His dad reckons he should see a doctor.'

Miss Marbles picked up a piece of broken flowerpot. 'Well,' she said. 'I think that's all I need to know.'

She held out her hand. 'Welcome to Mighty High, Stan.'

Stan shook hands uncertainly. 'You mean I passed?'

'Of course you passed. You can start on Monday.'

Stan looked at his mum.

'Well I don't know,' she said. 'If that's what you want, Stan?'

Stan nodded. 'Yes. I mean yes, please.'

Mrs Button still looked doubtful. 'I just have one more question,' she said. 'These capes you were talking about – do you get them from a special cape shop?'

Chapter 3
Low-flying Teacups

The following Monday, Stan found himself in a large, musty classroom with twenty or so other children. He hadn't known what to expect – would some of them have wings or three pairs of ears? – but most of them looked more or less normal.

He was sitting next to a dark-haired girl who had her notebook, pens, pencils and frisbee (frisbee?) lined up neatly on the desk in front of her. A boy with glasses hurried in, out of breath, and sat down on Stan's left.

'Toilet,' he muttered.

Glancing round, Stan recognised some of the faces he'd seen at registration. Two rows behind was Tank, a scowling boy who seemed too big for the chair he was sitting on.

Miss Marbles entered the room and put down an armful of books on her desk.

'Good morning, everyone,' she said, brightly.

'Good morning, Miss Marbles,' mumbled the class.

'Let's begin with a simple question,' she said. 'What makes a superhero? Anyone?'

Several hands shot up.

'Superpowers,' said the dark-haired girl.

'Nice teeth,' said someone else.

'Muscles.' Tank grinned, flexing his arms so that everyone could see how big and strong they were.

'Yes.' Miss Marbles nodded. 'These things are all important, but nobody becomes a superhero unless they are *willing to learn*. That is why you are here, children. Perhaps you imagine that becoming a superhero is as simple as learning to ride a bike. Let me tell you, it isn't.

It requires patience, dedication and the right kind of tights.'

The head teacher took off her glasses.

'And there is something else,' she said. 'You must learn to work together. Teamwork, children. Without teamwork you will achieve nothing. Which brings us neatly to the subject of our first lesson. I'd like you to get into groups of three or four.'

There was a buzz of excited voices. Stan looked around to find most of the class were quickly forming groups with their friends. He seemed to be the only one who didn't know anyone.

34

He felt a tap on his shoulder. It was the dark-haired girl.

'Looks as if you're stuck with me.' She grinned. 'I'm Minnie. It's my first day.'

'Mine too,' said Stan. 'I'm Stan, by the way.'

'I'm Miles, in case anyone's interested.'

They both turned to the boy with glasses, who was probably the least likely superhero Stan had ever seen. He had a pale face and bright-coloured braces on his teeth. *You wouldn't have bet on him in a fight*, thought Stan, *unless his opponent was a hamster*.

Miss Marbles wheeled in some kind of contraption. 'This is RAMM,' she explained. 'It stands for Random Aerial Missile Machine. Let me show you how it works.'

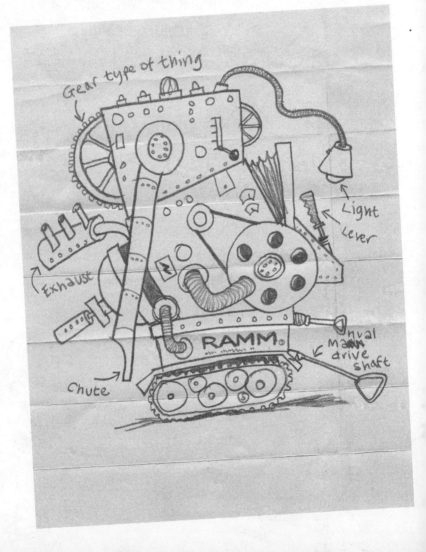

They gathered round to watch. Miss Marbles pulled a lever. Red lights flashed and the machine whirred and clunked into life. The chute suddenly jolted upwards.

KADODOOSH!!

A teacup shot across the room at ninety miles an hour. Miss Marbles smiled and switched off the machine.

'That might have been a thunderbolt, not crockery,' she said. 'As superheroes, you never know when you're going to be attacked. That's why you must always be alert and on your toes. Now, the object of this task is simple – to put RAMM out of action. Everyone understand? Splendid. Which group would like to go first?'

There was a deafening silence. No one seemed eager to brave a storm of ninety-mile-an-hour teacups. Stan felt a hand shove him in the back so that he stumbled forward.

'Ah, Stan,' said Miss Marbles. 'I see you're keen to make an impression on your first day.'

Stan turned to see Tank wearing a big stupid grin. No prizes for guessing who had volunteered him.

A few minutes later he was at the front next to Miles and Minnie, with his ears feeling as if they were on fire. He just hoped that he wouldn't make a total idiot of himself in front of the entire class.

'So how do you want to do this?' he asked Minnie.

She tucked her frisbee into her belt.

'You dodge the fire. I'll try to reach the machine and turn it off,' she said.

'OK.' Stan nodded. 'Sounds simple enough.'

'I wouldn't bet on it,' said Miles. 'If it's firing at ninety miles an hour, we've got about 0.4 seconds to react.'

'How did you work that out?' asked Stan.

'Just a rough guess.'

The rest of the class had moved to one side of the room, well out of the line of fire. Tank had climbed on to a desk so he could get a better view. He looked as if he was enjoying this.

'Ready?' said Miss Marbles.

Stan took a deep breath as Miss Marbles pushed the lever up to level four.

Something shot from the machine and whizzed past Stan's left ear. A dinner plate

smashed against the back wall. More missiles
followed in rapid fire. Random kitchen objects
were spitting out of the chute like bullets from
a machine gun. There was nothing Stan could

do. His ears were on red alert and burned every time he needed to duck. He raised his head for a second.

'Don't just stand there! Work together!

TEAMWORK!' Miss Marbles yelled above the din.

'It's too fast!' gasped Stan. 'What do we do?'

'We need a shield!' Miles shouted as another dinner plate whizzed past.

'Brilliant!' replied Stan. 'See any lying around?'

He glanced behind him. Come to think of it, lots of things could act as a shield: a chair, for instance. He rolled over and grabbed one, holding it in front of him.

'Good! Now you're thinking!' cried Miss Marbles.

A cereal bowl shattered against the chair. Minnie copied Stan's example and they closed ranks, sheltering behind their shields as objects zipped past them like bullets.

'Wait, I've got an idea,' said Minnie.

She pulled the frisbee from her belt.

Stan stared at her, wide-eyed. 'We haven't got time for games!'

'Just give me a few seconds,' said Minnie. 'I think I can put it out of action.'

Stan was baffled. Surely she'd gone mad. What did she have in mind – challenging the machine to a game of extreme frisbee? Minnie crouched on one knee and peeped out, dodging a flying fruit bowl. The next moment Stan saw her dart out into the open and draw back her throwing arm. The frisbee hummed through the air, curving towards the machine.

It struck its target with a loud thud, sending the control lever lurching to the left. There was a dull *clunk* and a *whirr* – followed by a sudden silence.

WOOOSH

Stan cautiously lowered the chair he was holding. The hailstorm of objects had dried up. Incredibly Minnie's deadly accurate frisbee had managed to put the machine out of action. The three of them got slowly to their feet and looked at the wreckage of broken crockery and bent spoons littering the room.

'Splendid! Well done!' cried Miss Marbles, starting to clap. The rest of the class joined in with the applause while Stan and his new friends stood there slightly dazed, like survivors of a shipwreck.

'Nice going,' said Stan.

'You too,' nodded Minnie.

Miles felt his head. 'It was nothing,' he said.

Chapter 4

Cabbage Surprise

Meanwhile, in the damp, dark kitchen below stairs, Mrs Sponge, the school cook, was preparing lunch for the staff and children. She was just stirring the soup (turnip and treacle) when there was a knock at the back door.

'Delivery,' said one of the men outside.

Mrs Sponge frowned. 'But I didn't order anything.'

'This is the address. I just do what I'm told,' he said. 'Crate of cabbages. Sign here.'

Two delivery men carried in a crate as big

as a fridge, panting and grunting with the effort. They dumped it in the middle of the kitchen floor and departed. Mrs Sponge stared at it and shook her head. It was probably some mistake at the suppliers, but she could always make something out of cabbages – cabbage stew for instance, or cabbage surprise. She went back to peeling turnips.

'Mother!'

Mrs Sponge looked around. There was no one there – only the damp walls. It must have been the door creaking, she decided, going back to her work.

'Mother, it's me!'

This time the voice made her jump. It seemed to come from the crate. She crept closer, clutching her ladle just in case.

'Hello?' she said in a whisper.

'Mother!'

Mrs Sponge gasped. The crate contained talking cabbages! They seemed to be under the impression she was their mother!

'Are you . . . are you all right?' she asked, speaking to the crate.

'Of course I'm not all right. I can't breathe!' snapped the cabbages 'Get me out!'

With trembling fingers, Mrs Sponge undid the catch and slowly lifted the lid. Inside were dozens of perfectly ordinary green cabbages. She poked one gingerly with her finger to see if it would speak. It didn't, but suddenly the entire top layer wobbled and a head rose up, sending cabbages bouncing across the floor like footballs.

'Shut up, Mother! It's me!'

Mrs Sponge stared in surprise. 'Kenneth?' she said. 'You scared me half to death. What are you doing in there?'

'What does it look like? I'm hiding.'

'In a crate of cabbages?'

'No, in a cheese and pickle sandwich. Help me out – my legs have gone to sleep.'

Mrs Sponge helped her son to climb

out of the crate. Close up, he didn't smell so great – like someone who'd spent far too long in the company of cabbages.

He stood up and stretched.

The effect would have been more impressive without the cabbage leaf on his head. It fell off as he stamped around the kitchen trying to get some feeling back into his legs.

'What are you doing here?' asked Mrs Sponge. 'You've never come before.'

'Mother, I've been in prison. They don't let you out at weekends.'

She tutted. 'Oh, Kenneth, have you been stealing sweets again?'

Her son rolled his eyes. 'How many times, Mother? I'm not six years old. I am the Green Meanie, internationally famous supervillain. Why do you think I'm dressed like this?'

'I don't know. Aren't you hot in that mask?

Anyway, you haven't answered my question: why are you here?'

'Where else was I to go?' said the Green Meanie. 'They're looking for me.'

The truth was he needed somewhere to lie low for a while. He'd spent almost a year in Darkmoor Prison after that meddling super-twerp Captain Courageous had foiled his plot to rob the Bank of England. (Who knew that place had burglar alarms?) Finally, after many attempts, he had escaped. It had cost him an entire night bumping around in the back of a lorry inside a box, but at last he was free. All he needed now was a suitable hideout, somewhere the police would never think to look for him.

'What are you doing in this dump?'

'It's my job,' replied his mother. 'Mighty High. I am cook and head dinner lady. Actually I'm the only dinner lady.'

The Green Meanie laughed meanly.

'You – a cook? You can't even make toast!'

'Don't be silly, dumpling, I don't make toast,' said Mrs Sponge. 'I make nice hot soups and stews. Are you hungry?'

'No, thanks,' said the Green Meanie. He had already looked into the saucepan, where turnip peelings were bubbling in a gloopy brown soup.

He glanced at the stairs. 'So, who else is here?'

'Just the staff and the children,' replied Mrs Sponge. 'Though I must say, they're a funny lot.'

'How do you mean?'

'Well, the things they do,' she said. 'The other day I saw one come in through a door.'

'What's funny about that?'

'The door was shut. And there's another who can change colour: red, green, blue – he's like a traffic light.'

'You're imagining things,' said the Green Meanie.

'Of course I'm not, you silly sausage.'

The Green Meanie frowned. Children who could walk through doors or change their skin colour? If it was true, there was only one explanation. These weren't ordinary brats, they were *super*-brats. He had stumbled on some sort of secret training school for superheroes. Mighty High – of course, the clue was in the name!

He paced up and down the kitchen. This was terrible, the worst news since the day he found out the Tooth Fairy didn't exist. It was bad enough that muddling fathead Captain Courageous saving the world every time you opened a newspaper. But now they were breeding a new race of superheroes – little, annoying ones who would bite your ankles. He had to get out of here, and quickly.

But wait, perhaps he didn't. Come to think of it, this was the answer to his problems – the perfect hideout. A school was the last place on earth the police would come looking for him! He could lie low and start planning his next attempt to take over the world. There was no reason the snivelling super-brats should get in his way. In fact, they might even turn out to be useful.

'Mother,' he said, 'does anyone else come down to the kitchen?'

'Not really, dumpling.'

'Good, then I'll be stopping here. You can make up a bed for me. And while you're about it, clean this place up – it stinks of cabbages.'

His mother stared. 'But, fruit drop, you can't stay here!'

'Why not?'

'Someone might see you. What if they discover you're, you know . . . the Green Moanie?'

'The Green *Meanie*!'

'Exactly,' said Mrs Sponge. 'If I'm caught sheltering an arch-criminal I'll lose my job.'

'Don't worry, Mother. You forget – I am a master of disguise,' said her son. 'No one will recognise me. And you never know – while I'm here I might even try my hand at teaching.'

'Don't be silly, dumpling,' said Mrs Sponge. 'What on earth could you teach children?'

'Oh, you'd be surprised,' said the Green Meanie with an evil smile.

Chapter 5
Unbeatable

Stan was worried. On the desk sat the various items Miss Stitch had said they would need for today's lesson: scissors, a tape measure, pins, and needle and thread. Somehow he had assumed that superhero costumes would be provided, but it turned out that they were expected to MAKE them.

Their teacher was a tiny, silver-haired woman who looked as if she could fit in someone's pocket. Right now she was reminding them of the importance of a well-fitting costume.

'What is the first thing you notice about a

superhero?' she asked. 'Is it their dazzling smile? Their broad shoulders? Is it the fact that they just crashed in through the skylight instead of using the door? No, what you notice first is what they're wearing. The costume tells you instantly that they're a superhero. Take away the cape, the mask, the skintight suit, and what would you be?'

'Naked, miss,' Tank shouted out. The class dissolved into giggles.

'That will do,' sighed Miss Stitch. 'Turn to your textbooks. In Chapter 4 you will find some useful tips on choosing your costume.'

Stan opened the large red book on his desk. He started to read . . .

DON'T BE GOOD, BE SUPER.

PROPERTY OF
MIGHTY HIGH SCHOOL

The Pocket Guide for Superheroes

Everything you need to know
to save the world.

4

DRESSED TO THRILL

For a superhero, nothing is more important than choosing the right costume. Well, OK, scratch that – avoiding a horrible death is more important. And saving the world from total destruction – and remembering your mum's birthday. But choosing the right costume is right up there with life's big decisions. Get it wrong like the Beige Anger and you will never be heard of again. (Never heard of the Beige Anger? Exactly.)

A good outfit will make an impact and get you in and out of burning buildings. A bad one will mean you're mistaken for a hot-dog seller. Here are some common errors you need to avoid.

1. MASKS

A mask creates an air of mystery. But don't fall into traps like these:

FIG 1 Over-elaborate mask

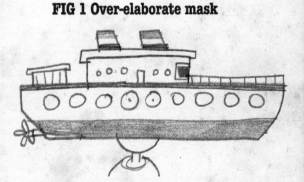

FIG 2 Who forgot the eyeholes????

FIG 3 Wrong sort of mask

2. CAPES

A superhero without a cape is like a hamburger without the ham. Capes are great for rippling in the wind when you are flying or just drying your hair.

Take care, though, over the length of your cape. Too short and it'll look as if you're wearing a napkin, too long and you'll run the risk of nasty accidents when using lifts or escalators.

FIG 4 Dangers of cape-related accidents

3. BOOTS

Boots should be knee-length, shiny and have a firm grip. Not too firm a grip, though.

This book belongs to Stanley Button

DON'T BE GOOD, BE SUPER.

MIGHTY HIGH SCHOOL

While Stan, Minnie and Miles were meant to be looking at the textbook, they talked in low voices.

'How did you learn to do that?' said Stan.

'Do what?' asked Minnie.

'Throw a frisbee like that. It was deadly.'

'I practise a lot,' said Minnie. 'My mum calls me Frisbee Kid. What does your mum call you?'

'Dangerboy, because of my ears,' said Stan.

'You've got dangerous ears?'

'No, I get this funny feeling when something's going to happen,' explained Stan. 'As if my ears are going crazy.' He scratched them out of habit. 'Anyway, what about you, Miles?'

'Me?' Miles's cheeks flushed. 'I can't do anything. I'm just ordinary.'

'You can't be,' said Minnie, 'or you wouldn't be here.'

'Well, OK.' Miles sighed. 'I know stuff.'

'What kind of stuff?' asked Stan.

'All kinds – dates, names, numbers, information – it just sort of sticks to my brain like chewing gum.'

'Wow!' said Stan. It sounded the complete opposite of his brain, where things just slipped through like sawdust. 'What's 24,372 divided by 40?' he asked.

'609.3,' answered Miles without even blinking.

'Mega!' said Stan. 'You didn't even use your fingers!'

He looked up. Mrs Stitch was talking again, but he'd missed most of what she'd said.

'And once you have all your measurements, you're ready to start,' she finished. 'Everyone clear?'

'Start what?' whispered Stan.

'Making our costumes,' replied Minnie. 'What's your favourite colour?'

'Blue,' said Stan.

'Brown,' said Miles.

'Mine's yellow, but I think we'll go with blue,' decided Minnie. 'Brown's a bit boring, and if we wear yellow we'll look like a bunch of bananas.'

'Er, who's we?' asked Stan.

'Us,' said Minnie. 'If we're going to be a team, we'll all need the same costume. Keep up.'

'Oh,' said Stan.

That seemed to settle the matter. Stan had never considered being one of a team, but now he thought about it, it was a pretty good idea. Being a superhero on your own was hard work. But if they were in a gang, they could go on daring missions together. Besides, Minnie seemed a lot more organised. Organisation had never been Stan's strong point – he was much better at things like panicking.

'So we'll need a name. What shall we call ourselves?' asked Minnie, as she ran a tape measure along Stan's arm.

It was a good question. Every superhero gang had its own name, usually something that sounded strong and dynamic, like the Magnetics or the Avengers.

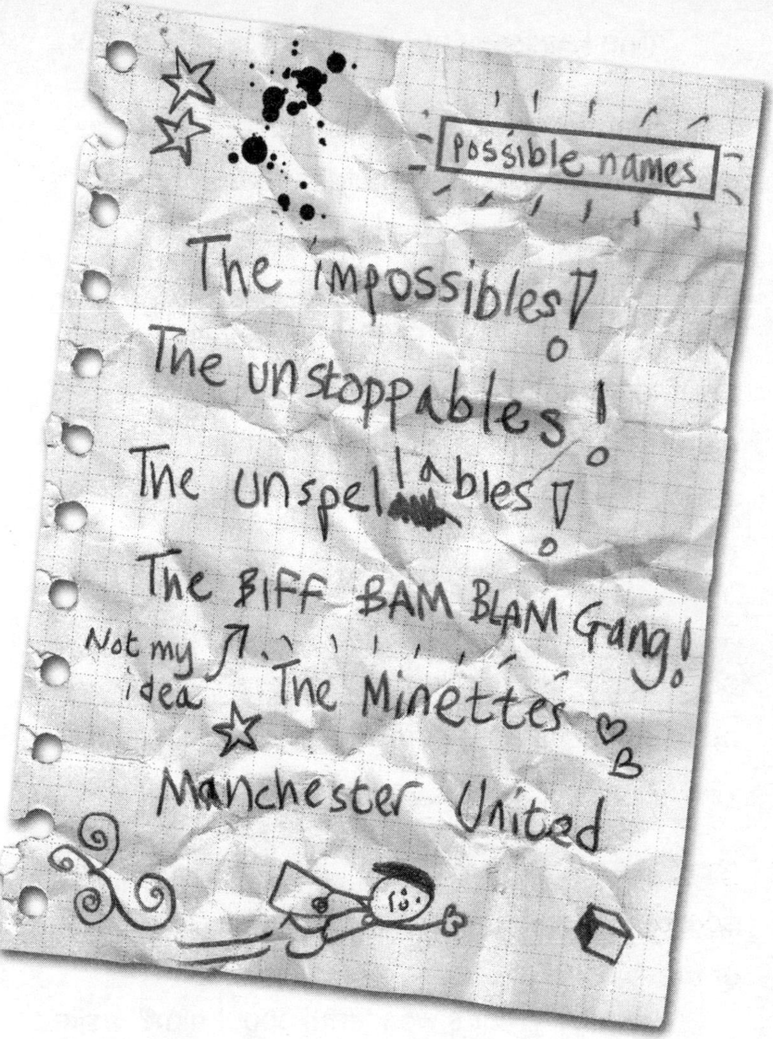

possible names

The impossibles

The unstoppables!

The unspellables

The BIFF BAM BLAM Gang!

Not my idea → The Minettes

Manchester United

But nothing seemed quite right.

'How about the Fearless Three?' asked Stan.

'The Fearless Four is better,' said Minnie.

Stan frowned. 'But we don't have four,' he said. 'There's you, me and Miles – that makes three.'

'Don't forget Pudding.'

'Pudding?'

'Yes. He's my dog.'

'You can't have a dog in a superhero gang!'

'Why not?'

'Because he's a dog!' said Stan. 'Name me one superhero who's a dog.'

'He's not just any dog,' said Minnie. 'He's *my* dog, and he's Pudding the Wonderdog.'

'Really? What's wonderful about him?' asked Miles.

'He's got X-ray vision. He knows if you've got a biscuit in your pocket.'

'All dogs can do that,' said Stan. 'And it's not going to be much use if we're fighting some evil mastermind.'

'Not unless he's got a biscuit in his pocket,' said Miles.

'But that's not all,' said Minnie. 'He can lie really still. You wouldn't even know he was there.'

Stan laughed. 'I bet I would!'

'OK, I'll prove it to you,' said Minnie. 'And if I do, Pudding's in the gang. Agreed?'

'OK,' agreed Stan.

Miles nodded. 'Fine by me.'

Minnie folded her arms. 'Look under the table,' she said.

'What?'

'Go on, take a look.'

Stan and Miles bent down and looked. They stared in disbelief.

'How did he get there?' asked Stan, amazed.

'That's one of his superpowers,' Minnie grinned. 'He's invisible to teachers. So we're all agreed then? Pudding's in?'

Stan sighed. He had a feeling he was going to regret this. But at that moment Miss Stitch, who had been flitting around the class, appeared in front of them.

'Well?' she said. 'What have you three
done? Let me see your work.'

Minnie showed her the list of measurements, which was as far as they'd managed to get.

Miss Stitch tutted and waggled her head, taking a pair of scissors from her top pocket. The next few minutes were a blur of movement as she measured, snipped and sewed pieces of material on a machine. When it was done she handed them three bright blue costumes. They put them on and squashed in front of the mirror on the wall to look.

The effect was astonishing. 'Wow!' gasped Miles. 'We look amazing – like real superheroes.'

'Incredible,' said Minnie.

'That's it!' said Stan. 'I know what we should call ourselves.'

'What?'

'The Invincibles!'

The Invincibles – it sounded good. The three of them stared at their reflections in the mirror with Pudding's head nosing in between their legs.

They had a name and costumes. All they needed now was to begin fighting Evil. But where did they start? *That's the trouble with living somewhere like Gormley*, thought Stan, *it's not exactly crawling with criminal masterminds*.

He needn't have worried, however, because at that very minute Evil was stalking the school corridor and was just about to knock on Miss Stitch's door.

DANGERBOY (aka Stan)

SPECIAL POWERS: Radar ears that sense danger

WEAPON OF CHOICE: Tiddlywinks

STRENGTHS: Survival against the odds

WEAKNESSES: Never stops worrying

SUPER RATING: 53

FRISBEE KID (aka Minnie)

SPECIAL POWERS: Deadly aim

WEAPON OF CHOICE: 'Frisbee anyone?'

STRENGTHS: Organised, bossy

WEAKNESSES: See above

SUPER RATING: 56

BRAINIAC (aka Miles)

SPECIAL POWERS: Super brainbox

WEAPON OF CHOICE: Quiz questions

STRENGTHS: Um . . .

WEAKNESSES: Hates to fight

SUPER RATING: 41.3

THE INVINCIBLES

PUDDING THE WONDERDOG

SPECIAL POWERS: Sniffing out treats

WEAPON OF CHOICE: Licking and slobbering

STRENGTHS: Obedience

WEAKNESSES: World class wimp

SUPER RATING: 2

Chapter 6
Criminal Science

Miss Marbles was looking at the *Gormley Gazette*. A short news article on page five had caught her eye.

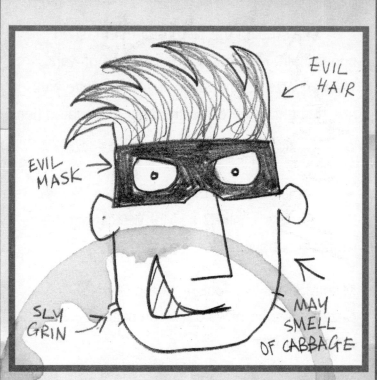

Police today issued this photofit picture of the Green Meanie, the power-mad arch-criminal who recently escaped from Darkmoor Prison where he was serving a three-year sentence for plotting to take over the world.

He is a master of disguise and extremely dangerous.

She studied the picture of the masked supervillain. He looked a nasty piece of work. *Thank goodness I'm never likely to run into him,* she thought. A knock on the door interrupted her.

'Yes? Come in!'

A tall, rake-thin man entered. As he folded himself into a chair, Miss Marbles caught a faint whiff of cabbage.

'Can I help you?' she asked.

'Actually, I think maybe *I* can help *you*,' he said with a sly smile. 'My name is Professor Von Hardbum.'

'Von what?' said Miss Marbles.

'Von Hardbum. I come from a long line of Hardbums. But I'm not here to discuss my family. I'll come straight to the point – I hear you are looking for a new teacher.'

Miss Marbles noticed her cat had run off.
She had a strange feeling that the visitor's smile
was familiar.

'I'm sorry,' she said. 'I have all the staff
I need right now. Besides, Mighty High is no
ordinary school.'

'I know.' Von Hardbum nodded. 'But then I'm
no ordinary teacher. I'm not one to boast, but I'm
probably the cleverest person in this room. I was
Visiting Professor at the University of Trowzerzhoff,
perhaps you've heard of it?'

'I don't think so. What did you teach?' asked
Miss Marbles.

'Teach?' The professor looked blank for a moment. 'Oh, yes, I taught many things. Mainly criminals . . . er, criminal science.'

'Goodness! How interesting!' said Miss Marbles. 'And what is that exactly?'

'It is, well . . . like science, only with criminals. For instance, we did an experiment to find out what happens if you keep them at temperatures below freezing.'

'What does happen?'

'They turn blue.'

The head teacher nodded thoughtfully. 'I'm afraid I'm no expert.'

'Not many people are,' said Von Hardbum with a sigh. 'That's why I want to teach children. You see, I've always dreamed of a place where little super-morons – I mean minors – could be taught the skills they'll need for the future.'

Miss Marbles' eyes shone. 'But that is

exactly what we aim to do here at Mighty High!'

'You don't say!'

'I do. Just think how we could change the
world if we trained
just fifty new
superheroes.'

'Imagine!'
said Von Hardbum,
grinding his teeth.

Miss Marbles
leaned forward
and clasped her
hands. 'You know,
come to think of it,
perhaps I am looking
for another teacher,'
she said.

'Look no further,' said
the professor.

'I'm afraid the school is

rather old,' Miss Marbles apologised. 'It may not be what you're used to.'

'Don't worry,' replied Von Hardbum. 'Compared to this, my last place was like a prison.'

They shook hands and Miss Marbles closed the door behind him. *What a pleasant young man*, she thought, *and a professor of criminal science too*. There was no doubt he would be able to teach the children all kinds of useful things.

Mrs Sponge hummed to herself as she headed to the dining hall carrying a large saucepan of lumpy mash.

'Psst!'

She looked round. This was getting annoying. She could hardly walk four steps today without hearing voices.

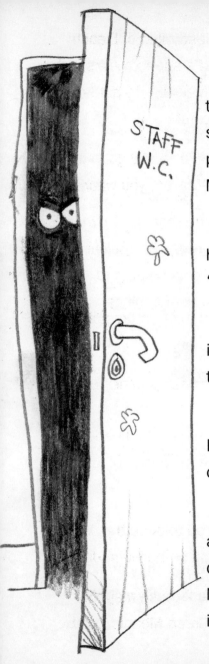

'Psst!'

It came from the staff toilet, where the door was slightly open and a face peeped through the crack. Mrs Sponge went closer.

'It's me, Mother,' hissed the Green Meanie. 'Get in here!'

'I'm not coming in there with you. It's a toilet,' said Mrs Sponge.

'Don't be ridiculous. Hurry up, before someone comes along!'

Mrs Sponge sighed and slipped inside the door, which the Green Meanie bolted on the inside. It wasn't an ideal place for a secret meeting – it smelled of bleach and was as cramped as an elf's shoebox. Mrs Sponge looked around for somewhere to put her saucepan and decided on the floor.

'Is this going to take long? I've still got a rice pudding to make,' she said. 'Why are you wearing those silly glasses?'

The Green Meanie took them off. 'It's my cunning disguise.'

His mother snorted. 'You think you're going to fool anybody like that?'

'As a matter of fact, your head teacher just gave me a job.'

Mrs Sponge stared. 'As a teacher?'

'Naturally.'

'But you hate children. You told me they were disgusting maggots who should be boiled in oil.'

'You're forgetting, Mother – these maggots have superpowers,' said the Green Meanie. 'With the right sort of guidance, who knows what they could do?'

'You mean one day they could be superheroes?' asked Mrs Sponge.

The Green Meanie raised his eyebrows. 'Or supervillains,' he said.

Mrs Sponge sat down heavily on the only available seat, which was the toilet.

'Why not? Think of it,' said the Green Meanie. 'With an army of super-brats, I could do anything. I could rid the world of fat-headed do-gooders like Captain Courageous. I would be unstoppable! MWUH HA! HA! HA!'

His evil laugh was cut short by an unpleasant sensation. Looking down, he realised he had trodden in a saucepan of mashed potato. He removed his foot with a sucking sound.

'Now look what you've done, you big clumsy!' scolded his mother, scraping lumpy mash back into the pan. 'In any case, aren't you forgetting something?'

'What?'

'Miss Marbles. She's head teacher of this school.'

'Not for much longer,' said the Green Meanie. 'I have other plans for Miss Marbles. Come with me!'

They hurried through corridors, with the supervillain leaving a trail of mashed potato and his mother trying to keep up, slowed down by the heavy pan. Finally they stopped outside a room with a black door.

The Green Meanie unlocked the door and went inside. The room was dark and shadowy and the shutters were drawn. Scientific apparatus bleeped and whirred while a faint humming sound filled the air. On the lab desk sat something covered by a dusty old sheet.

'Are you ready?' asked the Green Meanie.

'Yes, but hurry up. I told you, I've got a rice pudding to make,' grumbled his mother.

'Then feast your eyes on this!'

The Green Meanie whipped off the sheet.

Mrs Sponge peered at the strange device on the desk. 'You've dragged me all the way down here just to show me a hairdryer?' she said.

'Of course it's not a hairdryer,' snapped the Green Meanie. 'It's something I've been working on in secret for years. I call it . . .

THE GIGANTINATOR!'

Mrs Sponge picked up the device to examine it more closely. 'What does this switch do?' she asked.

'DON'T TOUCH THAT!' cried her son, snatching it back. 'Stand over there and I'll show you. Now, let's see – what shall we use as a specimen?'

He looked around the lab and his eye fell on a tiny bluebottle which had landed on the mashed potato stuck to his foot. Taking a glass beaker he brought it down swiftly over the fly, trapping it inside. It buzzed against the glass, trying to escape.

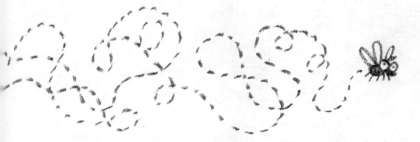

'Now, my beauty,' leered the Green Meanie, 'how would you like to take part in a little experiment?'

He switched on the Gigantinator and took careful aim. Immediately the humming in the room grew louder. Mrs Sponge covered her ears and backed away as her power-crazed son turned the dial and the volume increased.

Bolts of blue light fizzed and crackled through the air as the beaker started to shake . . .

Chapter 7

Hairy Scary

Stan was staring hard at a brown egg on a plate.

'You're not doing it right,' said Minnie. 'You've got to concentrate.'

'How can I concentrate with you talking in my ear?' complained Stan.

He bent down until his eyes were level with the egg and scowled at it furiously. Miss Marbles had told them that anything could be controlled using mind power, so their first task was to move an egg without touching it. So far none of the class had got anywhere, although Tank had managed to make scrambled egg when he sat down.

NOT MOVING ↘

Stan groaned. 'This is impossible!'

'Actually it's not,' Miles informed him.
'Lots of superheroes can do it. It's called telekinesis.'

'Well, you have a go, if you know so much,' said Stan.

Miles changed places with him. He took off his glasses and squatted down.

'See! It wobbled!' he cried excitedly.

'Only because you jogged the table,' said Minnie. 'You're not meant to lean on it.'

Miles moved back a little and went back to staring.

'Concentrate really hard,' said Stan.

'I'm trying. Stop humming, will you?' said Miles.

Stan frowned. 'I'm not humming.'

'Well, somebody is.'

'Don't look at me,' said Minnie.

They all listened. Stan could hear it now – a low hum, though actually it was more like a buzz. More worryingly still, his ears were starting to prickle. He glanced around the room.

'Something's wrong,' he said.

'You're telling me! Your ears have gone bright pink,' said Minnie.

'They do that. We need to get out of here,' said Stan, looking towards the door.

The buzzing had grown louder, so loud that other people had noticed it. They were looking around with puzzled expressions. Miss Marbles checked the light switch. The noise, however, seemed to be coming from outside the room.

Something banged on the door, startling them all.

'Yes? Come in!' said Miss Marbles.

The door jumped on its hinges.

'I said, *come in*!' the head teacher repeated. 'Tank, go and open the door, will you?'

'NO!' warned Stan. 'Miss, it might be dangerous!'

'Don't be ridiculous,' said Miss Marbles.

The door sounded as if it was about to splinter in pieces. The buzzing was deafening now, filling the room. Tank had reached the door and turned the handle. He leapt back with a yell as something huge zoomed past his head and into the room.

Chaos broke out as children screamed and fled, diving under the tables, smashing plates and eggs. Only Miss Marbles remained rooted to the spot, staring upwards.

Stan found himself squashed under a desk with Miles and Minnie. They could hear the giant creature buzzing backwards and forwards like a low-flying plane.

'What *is* that thing?' panted Stan.

'I didn't get a close look,' replied Miles, 'but it's probably a common housefly or bluebottle. Don't worry – they're usually harmless.'

'They're not usually *that* big!' said Minnie.

The noise had suddenly stopped. Stan poked his head above the table to see if the monster insect had buzzed off. It hadn't. It had settled on Miss Marbles' desk, where it seemed to be planning its next move. Stan could see its horrible hairy legs and red eyes as big as dinner plates. Across the room he spotted Miss Marbles flattened against the wall, trying to inch her way slowly to the door. He guessed she meant to escape and raise the alarm. But to reach the door she'd have to get past the giant fly.

Stan ducked down, his heart racing.

'We have to do something,' he said. 'Miss Marbles is trapped.'

Miles stared at him. 'Are you mad? What can we do?'

'I thought you said it was only a bluebottle,' Minnie reminded him.

'A GIANT bluebottle,' said Miles. 'It probably eats spiders for breakfast.'

Stan had an idea. 'Wait,' he said. 'What do flies eat?'

'What?'

'You're the brainbox – what do flies eat?'

Miles tried hard to think. 'All kinds of stuff,' he said eventually. 'Sugar, biscuits, anything.'

'What about sticky stuff?' said Stan.

'I don't know – probably.' Miles nodded.

Stan looked out again. Miss Marbles hadn't got any closer to the door. Her way was blocked by a large heavy bookcase. There was no sign of the fly. Looking up, Stan saw it on the ceiling, crawling around like a bloated blue-black beetle. Any moment now it might swoop down and carry the head teacher off.

They would have to move fast. He turned to Minnie. 'Grab as many eggs as you can and aim for its head,' he told her. 'Miles, you come with me!'

'Can't I stay here?'

'Come on!'

109

They dashed out. At the same moment the monster fly took off from the ceiling.

It swooped down like a bomber plane. Miss Marbles screamed. Minnie took aim.

SPLAT!

An egg splatted the fly on the side of the head.

SPLAT!
SPLODGE!
SPLAT!

Stunned, the insect dropped to the floor. Gloopy yellow yolk dripped from its head and trickled into its eyes. It staggered a little, buzzing like an untuned radio. Then it rubbed its front legs together and started to feed.

'NOW!' cried Stan. He and Miles heaved with all their strength. The heavy bookcase swayed and toppled forwards.

There was a short silence.

'EWWW!' cried Minnie, pulling a face.

Slowly, the rest of the class crept out from their hiding places and stared at the sticky yellow puddle spreading across the floor. Two black hairy legs stuck out from under the bookcase. Miss Marbles sank into a chair, panting for breath, and wiped some egg off her face.

'Thank you, Stan,' she groaned. 'I knew that bookcase would come in handy one day. Now perhaps someone would fetch Mr Bounds –'

But Minnie interrupted. She was staring through the open door into the hallway. 'Miss Marbles,' she said, 'you might want to look at this.'

Chapter 8
Written in Peas

The class followed Miss Marbles into the corridors where they stood and stared, open-mouthed. A message was daubed in large green letters on the wall:

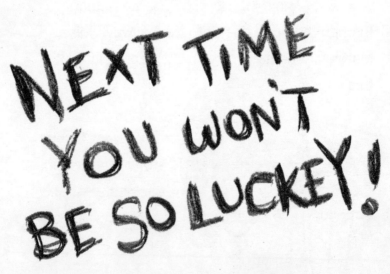

NEXT TIME YOU WON'T BE SO LUCKEY!

By now several other teachers had arrived, alerted by the noise. They all crowded around the wall, gazing at its grim message.

'This is terrible!' cried Mr Bounds, the PE teacher. 'Shocking!'

'Yes, I've never seen such spelling!' agreed Miss Stitch. 'Did one of you write this?'

The children all shook their heads. Miss Marbles was examining the writing.

'What is this stuff?' she asked, dabbing at it. She sniffed her finger, then tasted it.

'Peas,' she said. 'Mushy peas. There's only one person who could have done this.'

'A vegetarian?' said Miss Stitch.

'No, the Green Meanie. Look at this in today's paper.'

She produced the article that she'd saved from that morning.

Miss Stitch read it out. '"Police today issued this picture of the Green Meanie – the power-mad super-criminal who escaped from Darkmoor Prison . . ." Good heavens! Do you think this was his work, Headmistress?'

'Who else would write a death threat in mushy peas?' said Miss Marbles.

The newspaper cutting was passed around from hand to hand so that everyone could see the picture.

'YUCK!' said Stan. 'He's certainly ugly.'

'Actually,' said a voice, 'I'm told that he's rather handsome.'

They all turned round to see a tall man wearing green glasses, who had just arrived. He had brought Mrs Sponge, the dinner lady.

'Ah, this is Professor Von Hardbum,' said Miss Marbles. 'We're very lucky that he's going to be joining us at Mighty High.'

Miles nudged Stan. 'Von Hardbum?' he sniggered.

'He looks kind of creepy to me,' said Minnie.

Miss Marbles pointed to the message on the wall. 'What do you make of this, Professor?' she asked. 'Have you had anything to do with the Green Meanie?'

'As a matter of fact, I know all about him,' replied the professor.

'So you should,' muttered Mrs Sponge.

The professor shot her an icy glare. 'Haven't you got work to do?' he asked, pointedly. '*In the kitchen?*'

'Well, that depends,' grumbled Mrs Sponge. 'Are we having lunch today or not?'

Miss Marbles shook her head. 'I'm sorry, Mrs Sponge, but we're really rather busy right now,' she said. 'I'd like everyone to gather in the hall.'

Everyone crowded into the main school hall. Stan took his place with his friends in one of the front rows, where he'd get a good view. He felt a thrill of anticipation.

It was only his first day, but already he'd helped to disarm a Random Aerial Missile Machine and survived an attack from a giant fly. It was certainly more exciting than listening to Mr Horrocks recite the seven times table.

Miss Marbles spoke briefly about the importance of remaining calm under pressure,

119

then handed over to the new professor of criminal science. Von Hardbum clicked a button on a remote control and a large picture of the Green Meanie appeared on a screen.

'Take a good look,' said Von Hardbum. 'This is the evil genius you are up against – probably one of the greatest criminals of all time.'

Miles raised his hand. 'How come I've never heard of him?' he said.

'Because you are a small boy with the brain of a woodlouse,' replied the professor. 'Now, if I may continue, what do we know about this master villain? Firstly, that he's diabolically clever; second, that he's a master of disguise; third, that he's never yet been captured.'

A hand shot up. Miles again. 'I thought the paper said he escaped from prison.'

'Yes, well, all right, if you're going to be picky, Mister Smartypants, he was captured once,' said the professor. 'But that was down to bad luck and getting my . . . umm . . . his cape caught in a revolving door.'

The professor pointed to the picture on the screen. 'Supervillains do not look like everyone else. Note the mask, green bodysuit and impressive cape – these things should give you a clue. But as I said before, he is a master of disguise. He could be dressed as a window cleaner or an ice-cream salesman. He might even be your grandma. Trust no one, suspect everyone.'

Stan found himself looking round at the faces in the hall.

'Thank you, Professor,' said Miss Marbles, taking over. 'It goes without saying that we all need to be on our guard. The Green Meanie has attacked us here once and he's threatened to strike again. I want two members of staff patrolling the grounds at all times. Report to me anyone who looks suspicious – especially if they're wearing a mask. Professor, you

DON'T BE GOOD.
BE SUPER

THE GREEN MEANIE

DESCRIPTION: Lean, green, mean

SPECIAL POWERS: Power over vegetables

AMBITION: World domination – or failing that his own reality TV show

STRENGTHS: Diabolically clever, master of disguise

WEAKNESSES: None

SUPER EVIL RATING: 62
(appeal pending)

wanted to say something?'

'Yes, Headmistress,' said Von Hardbum. 'If I can make a suggestion, why wait for him to come to you?'

'I'm sorry, I don't follow,' said Miss Marbles.

'Well, look around,' said the professor. 'All these bright young superheroes, eager to make their mark. Why not send them out? Let them track down this villain and bring him to justice.'

Stan raised his hand. 'But what if he's here?' he said. 'Hiding in the school?'

Von Hardbum laughed uneasily. 'Oh, I hardly think that's likely.'

'Why not?' said Mrs Sponge. 'He might have arrived by cabbage.'

The professor silenced her with a glare. 'Believe me, this is the last place he'd be. If I know the Green Meanie, he's out there somewhere hiding in his secret lair.'

It wasn't long before Miss Marbles was busy organising all the pupils into groups and mapping out areas of the town for them to search. Stan, Miles and Minnie waited until it was their turn.

'Ah, Stan,' said the head teacher, 'I have a very special job for you and your friends.'

'Really?' said Stan. 'Should we wear our new costumes?'

Miss Marbles smiled. 'Well, that's up to you,' she said. 'They might get a bit dirty.'

Chapter 9
Sticky

Miles rinsed out his mop into the bucket. 'It's not fair,' he grumbled. 'Why pick on us?'

'If you did more mopping and less moaning, we might get finished,' said Minnie.

Stan swept bits of eggshell into a pile. When Miss Marbles said she had an important job for them, he hadn't expected it to be cleaning up the classroom. The rest of the school were out in the town hunting the Green Meanie, which sounded a lot more exciting than washing congealed egg and squashed fly off a sticky floor.

'I wonder where that fly came from,' he said.

Miles shrugged. 'Flies get everywhere.'

'Yes, but how did it grow so big?' asked Stan.

'Don't ask me,' said Miles. 'Maybe it ate too much cake.'

'You can't get that big just by eating cake.'

'You haven't met my gran,' said Miles.

Minnie turned to face them. For the last five minutes she had been staring anxiously out of the window. 'Has anyone seen Pudding?' she asked.

'No, why?' said Stan.

'I left him in the playground, but I can't see him.'

'I wouldn't worry,' said Stan. 'He's probably off chasing a cat or something,' said Stan.

'He's scared of cats.'

'Oh. Well, anyway, the gates are locked. What could happen to him?'

Down in the kitchen a large saucepan of rice pudding bubbled and hissed on the stove. The Green Meanie pulled on his mask and turned round, whirling his cape.

'How do I look?' he asked.

'Like a big green gooseberry,' said Mrs Sponge. 'Give me a kiss!'

'Get off, Mother!' scowled the supervillain. 'There's no time to lose. They're all out on the streets looking for me.'

'But you're not on the streets, sugar lump,' said his mother.

'Of course I'm not. That was just my cunning trick to get them out of the way. Now there's no one left but Miss Marbles. Heh heh heh!'

'Well, and me,' said Mrs Sponge.

'Yes, OK, and you.'

'And those three children I saw just now.'

'WHAT?' cried the Green Meanie. 'I thought they'd all gone out.'

'Well, I thought so too, buttercup, but I just passed them upstairs, mopping the floor.'

'Curses!' muttered the Green Meanie. 'Very well, I will deal with them later.'

Mrs Sponge added more pepper to the rice pudding. 'Now, dumpling, you're not going to do anything naughty, are you?' she asked.

'Don't be stupid, Mother. Pass me the Gigantinator.'

Mrs Sponge hunted around, finally locating the device underneath a damp tea towel. She wiped it down and handed it to her son.

'I hope we're not having any more flies,' she said. 'They spread germs.'

'Don't worry,' said the Green Meanie. 'The fly was just a warning, a little taste of what's to come. This time that halfwit headmistress won't escape so easily.'

'But, bunnikins, surely you're not actually going to harm her?'

The Green Meanie waved a gloved hand. 'Well, of course not, Mother. *I'm* not going to harm anyone. Now, what shall it be this time? A spider? No, something bigger, I think . . .' He raised a hand. 'Wait! What was that?'

'The rice pudding?' said Mrs Sponge.

'No, not that – someone's coming!' snapped the Green Meanie. 'Quick, hide! No, on second thoughts, I'll hide. You stand there and try to act normal.'

He slipped behind the door and waited. Mrs Sponge grabbed a fish slice and stood with it raised like a dagger, trying to look normal. Both of them held their breath and listened.

Someone was coming down the stairs. Whoever it was, they were trying to tread softly but not making a very good job of it. The Green Meanie heard small thumps and creaks, followed by the sound of panting. He gripped the Gigantinator, though it wasn't much use in the circumstances. If it was the police, one blast from its deadly rays would transform them into giant constables with size-22 feet.

The small thumps came on, then stopped.
He could hear the intruder right outside the door,
breathing heavily. Mrs Sponge backed away,
fighting an urge to scream. The door swung open
slowly.

Something padded into the room and stood there with its tongue hanging out.

'Oh, look!' cooed Mrs Sponge, squatting down. 'The little sausage! He must be lost.'

The Green Meanie came out from behind the door. 'Indeed,' he said. 'How fortunate he found his way down here. Shut the door, Mother.'

There was an evil look in his eye. He fiddled with the Gigantinator, turning the dial from BIG to EXTRA BIG to GIGANTIC.

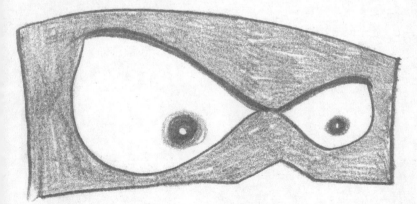

His mother looked at him. 'Bunnikins! You wouldn't!'

Minnie's voice echoed down the corridor. The three Invincibles had been searching for half an hour, but there was no sign of their fourth member.

Stan sighed. 'He could be anywhere. Maybe he's gone home.'

'He never goes home – not without me,' said Minnie.

'I expect he's hungry,' said Miles. 'I am.'

There was still no sign of lunch, or of Mrs Sponge who always served it in the dining hall. With everyone out in the town, the school suddenly seemed deserted. Minnie opened a door and glanced around the empty classroom before shutting it again.

'I don't see what you're so worried about,' said Stan. 'You keep saying he's a wonderdog.'

'He is,' replied Minnie, 'but he gets scared if I'm not with him.'

'Scared of what?'

'Well, spiders for one thing.'

'Spiders?' said Miles.

'Not just spiders. Squirrels, sparrows, doorbells, thunder, alarm clocks – he's sensitive.'

'He's a nutter,' muttered Miles.

Stan had gone ahead of them and was kneeling down to examine something on the floor. He rubbed his left ear, which was itching. 'Does Pudding have big feet?' he asked.

'No. Why?'

'This mark looks a bit like a dog's paw print. But it can't be – it's way too big.'

Further on they found evidence of more muddy prints like the first one. They seemed to be heading in the direction of the main hall. Stan scratched his ear again.

'I wish you'd stop doing that,' said Miles.

'Sorry, I can't help it,' said Stan. 'It itches. Maybe we should get Miss Marbles.'

'What for?' asked Minnie.

'I don't know. I've just got a bad feeling.'

'It's only Pudding. Surely you're not scared.'

'Of course not,' said Stan. 'It's just that my ears are nervous.'

Minnie rolled her eyes. 'Well, you can fetch Miss Marbles if you want to, but I'm going to find Pudding,' she said, marching off towards the hall. Stan and Miles looked at each other and then hurried after her. They hadn't gone far

when a deafening noise stopped them in their tracks.

'Was that a dog? It didn't sound like a dog,' said Miles.

But Minnie had heard it and set off at a run. Stan and Miles caught up with her as she burst into the hall. They all froze.

'Uh-oh!' said Stan. 'This can't be good.'

Pudding turned his enormous head to look at them. He was no longer a small, brown shaggy dog. Now he was a HUGE brown shaggy dog, big as a Bengal tiger and twice as hungry. His lead trailed on the floor.

'GRRRRR!' he snarled.

'Puddie Puds?' gulped Minnie. 'Have you been eating too many biscuits again?'

Pudding took a step towards them, but the lead round his neck pulled tight. A tall masked figure stepped out of the shadows. He was dressed in green from head to toe and wearing a long cape that swept to the floor. In one hand he grasped Pudding's leash and in the other he held something that looked like a deadly ray gun, or possibly a hairdryer. A faint smell of cabbage hung around him.

'YOU!' said Stan. 'You're the one in the paper – the Green Mintie!'

'The Green Meanie!' snapped the masked villain. 'Yes, you fools, it is I, the Count of Crime, number forty-four on the Darklord list of most wanted supervillains of all time.'

'What have you done to Pudding?' cried Minnie.

'Pudding?' said the Green Meanie. 'Perhaps you mean Fang, my new pet.'

'He's not called Fang,' said Minnie bravely.

'He's my dog and he only listens to me.'

'Is that so?' The Green Meanie smiled coldly. 'Let's find out, shall we?'

He let go of Pudding's leash and pointed a finger. 'GET THEM, FANG!' he snarled.

Pudding bounded forward with a low growl that didn't sound too friendly. 'GRRRRR!'

The hairs stood up on the back of Stan's neck and his ears burned as he backed towards the door.

'Stan,' croaked Miles, 'I think we should . . . you know . . .'

RUN!

'Exactly.'

They turned and ran. Stan made it to the corridor first, skidding on the slippery floor.

Bricks and plaster came tumbling down as the monster dog burst from the hall, taking the door with him. Stan swerved right and hurtled through the next pair of doors, running for his life.

Suddenly a hand appeared from nowhere and grabbed his arm. It sent him sprawling into a room where seconds later Minnie and Miles landed on top of him.

'OWW! OOOOF!'

There was a click of a key turning in a lock and someone turned round to face them.

Chapter 11
A Brilliant Plan

'Miss Marbles, it's you!' said Stan.

'Of course it's me! Now, will one of you please explain what on earth is going on?' said the head teacher.

'It's Pudding!' panted Minnie. 'He's a giant and he's chasing us!'

Miss Marbles looked confused. 'You're being chased by a giant pudding?'

'No, no, Pudding is my dog,' said Minnie.

'Then why is he chasing you?'

Together they explained as quickly as possible. Miss Marbles listened, fiddling with her glasses, as her expression grew more and more worried.

'You mean the Green Meanie is here?' she said. 'Are you sure?'

'Yes, we just saw him.' Stan nodded. 'He's out there now . . .'

A loud crash made them jump. There was the sound of breaking glass and a series of thuds and bangs from further down the corridor. Pudding was on the move, sniffing them out.

'MISS MARBLES?' called a loud voice.

The head teacher put a finger to her lips.

'I know you're hiding somewhere,' called out the Green Meanie. 'Give yourself up and I promise you the children will go free.'

Stan shook his head. 'Don't trust him,' he whispered.

There was a crash that sounded like a wall falling down.

'I don't think we have much choice,' said Miss Marbles.

'Maybe we do,' said Miles. 'Look at this!'

He had picked up a copy of **The Pocket Guide for Superheroes** from Miss Marbles' desk. It was open at Chapter 15 . . .

15

HOW TO FIGHT A BLOOD-CRAZED MONSTER AND LIVE

Face it, we've probably all been in this situation at one time or another. One minute you're walking down the street thinking about cream buns, the next you're facing a three-headed, bug-eyed beast who wants to eat you alive.

The crucial thing to remember when coming across a crazed monster is, DON'T PANIC. First, look at the facts . . .

1. Monsters are bigger than you.
   (The clue is in the word 'monster'.)

2. Monsters are stronger than you.

3. Monsters' main hobbies are roaring, tearing and devouring. Throwing them a stick to chase isn't going to work – and believe me, I've tried it.

So what can you do? Here are a few things that can work . . .

A. Run.

B. Hide.

C. Run AND hide.

D. Think of a brilliant foolproof plan.

Sadly, D is the point where many superheroes come unstuck. All I can say is, good luck, and remember: the bigger they are, the harder they fall.

'Huh! Fat lot of help that is,' said Miles, slamming the book shut.

'But it's right,' said Stan. 'All we need is a brilliant plan!'

'Oh well, why didn't you say so before?' said Miles.

But Stan was pacing up and down, talking excitedly. 'Remember that thing the Green Meanie had in his hand?' he said.

'Pudding's dog lead?' asked Minnie.

'No, the other thing. It looked like some sort of super-gizmo. I bet that's what made the fly gigantic.'

'You mean he used it on Pudding too?' said Minnie.

'Exactly.' Stan nodded. 'So don't you see? It's simple. All we need to do is get our hands on that gizmo.'

'And how do we do that exactly?' asked Minnie.

Stan turned to the head teacher. 'We'll need to borrow your glasses, and a dress, miss,' he said. 'Oh, and a wig – if you've got one.'

Chapter 12
Dog-gone

Five minutes later, the three Invincibles slipped
out into the shadowy corridor. There was no
sign of the monster Pudding or his sinister new
master. They crept forward cautiously, all except
for Miles, who was making enough noise to wake
the dead.

'Can't you walk more quietly?' hissed Stan.

'It's these shoes,' grumbled Miles. 'Why am I
the one that has to dress up?'

'Stop complaining,' said Minnie. 'I think you
look very pretty – doesn't he, Stan?'

'Very,' agreed Stan. 'If I was a short-sighted

154

teacher, I might even fancy you.'

Miles scowled and straightened his wig. He was tottering along like a giraffe on roller skates.

'I still don't see how this is going to help,' he moaned.

'I told you, it's Miss Marbles he wants,' said Stan. 'So you'll be able to get close to him.'

'I don't want to get close,' said Miles.

'You'll be fine,' said Stan. 'Don't worry – we'll be right behind you.'

Miles sighed. As plans went, this one wasn't the most brilliant he'd ever heard.

Stan held up his hand. His ears had begun to tingle . . .

KERBLAAMM!

The next moment, a wall at the far end of the corridor collapsed in a heap of rubble. Pudding's enormous head appeared through the jagged hole he'd made. He clambered over the bricks and emerged into the corridor, dragging the Green Meanie, who was trying to hold on to his lead.

'Uh-oh,' murmured Miles. 'Don't look now, but here they come.'

'Don't panic,' said Stan. 'Remember, superheroes don't run away if they've got a foolproof plan.'

'You try running in these shoes,' muttered Miles.

Pudding lumbered on, his huge shaggy body practically filling the corridor. His tail wagged, causing a picture to crash off the wall with a shattering of glass.

The Green Meanie pulled at the lead, holding Pudding back. 'Not yet, my pretty. All in good time,' he purred.

The two parties came to a halt, facing each other about twenty paces apart.

'So, Miss Marbles, you decided to come?' sneered the Green Meanie.

Stan nudged Miles. 'That's you, idiot! Say something!'

'Umm, hi, how are you?' squeaked Miles in a high-pitched voice.

The Green Meanie narrowed his eyes suspiciously. There was something odd about the head teacher. She seemed to have shrunk since his interview, and her hair looked like a bird's nest. No matter – soon he would be rid of the old bat and he could put his master plan into operation.

First he'd take over Mighty High and rename it the Meanie School of Evil. Once he had weeded out all the simpering weaklings, he'd begin to train his army of supervillains – and that would just be the start. Soon he would rule this pathetic town, the whole country, and eventually . . .

THE WORLD!

'Pardon?' said Stan.

'Just my evil joke,' said the Green Meanie. 'Now, why don't you kiddies run along straight back to your class and leave the grown-ups to settle this?'

'Never,' said Stan. 'We are the Invincibles and we're here to stop you.'

'Oh, please, spare me the heroic speeches,' said the Green Meanie with a sigh. 'Just hand over Miss Marbles and no one will get hurt.'

Stan considered. 'You promise?'

'Scout's honour,' said the Green Meanie.

Stan turned to Miles and lowered his voice. 'Remember, all you've got to do is grab that gizmo.'

'But what about Pudding?' said Miles.

The Green Meanie folded his arms impatiently. 'I'm waiting! I will count to three. One . . .'

'Go on,' said Stan.

'Two . . .'

Miles gulped and tottered forward on his high heels, with his heart thumping. He could see Pudding waiting hungrily for him up ahead, straining on his lead. At that moment Miles wished he had the kind of superpowers that were actually useful – invisibility, for instance. He stopped.

'Well?' he said. 'You promised no one would get hurt – Scout's honour.'

'So I did,' smiled the Green Meanie. 'But I was thrown out of the scouts.'

He loosened his grip on the dog's lead.

'Supper time, Fang!' he declared.

Pudding bounded forwards, free at last. Miles backed away as a blast of hot doggy breath hit him in the face.

'Stan, do something!' cried Minnie.

Pudding lowered his head, opened his huge jaws and . . .

SLURP!

Miles wiped the doggy slobber from his face.

'You dopey, moth-eaten mongrel!' raged the Green Meanie. 'I said "Get him!", not "Lick him!"'

'I told you he was my dog,' said Minnie.

'So, Mr Meanpants, it looks as if your evil plan has failed,' said Stan.

'Fools!' snarled the Green Meanie. 'You think you can defeat me – the greatest supervillain of all time? Not while I still have this!'

'A hairdryer?'

'Don't be stupid. This is the Gigantinator. All I have to do is turn the dial like this and I can make anything monster-sized. Heh heh heh!'

'Wicked!' said Stan. 'What if you turn it the other way?'

'I've never tried,' snapped the Green Meanie.

'No, you're right,' Stan agreed. 'It might be too evil.'

'Ha! We'll see about that!'

'Pudding!' cried Minnie, holding out her arms. He bounded up to her, wagging his tail.

The Green Meanie stared. Once again he'd been tricked, and this time by a bunch of snivelling super-brats. The one in the dress had even lost his wig. Still, he wasn't finished yet. He still had his brilliant invention.

Suddenly a frisbee zipped out of nowhere and struck his hand, sending the Gigantinator spinning from his grasp.

Stan was the first to grab it. 'Now,' he said, taking aim. 'I wonder what happens if I press *this* button.'

The world-famous supervillain backed away.

'No!' he said. 'Wait . . . let's talk about this . . .'

Chapter 13
Hairy

The following day, the Invincibles were called into Miss Marbles' office.

'Well,' said the head teacher, putting down the phone, 'I think that about wraps it up. I've just spoken to the police and given them a detailed description of the Green Meanie.'

'I still don't know how he managed to get away,' said Stan. 'One minute he was there, the next he'd gone.'

'I wouldn't worry. I'm sure he won't have got far,' said Miss Marbles. 'The main thing is that his evil plan failed and, thanks to you three,

167

the school is safe. We can go on with our vital mission of training the superheroes of the future. In fact, that's why I wanted to see you. I think the least you deserve is a reward.'

'A reward?' said Stan, leaning forward eagerly.

'Indeed,' said Miss Marbles, reaching into a drawer of her desk. 'That's why I asked Mrs Sponge to bake you this very special cake.'

She brought out a lopsided greenish-brown sponge. Cutting them each a fat slice, she handed them round.

'Mmm . . . urgh . . . umm,' said Stan, chewing with some difficulty.

Minnie pulled a face and spat out a soggy leaf on to her plate. 'Ugh! What's in it?' she asked.

'I'm not exactly sure,' said Miss Marbles. 'I think it was a new recipe, something like chocolate cabbage cake.'

Stan and his friends all looked sick and put down their plates.

'By the way,' continued Miss Marbles, 'I found this hairdryer on my desk.'

They all jumped up. 'Miss,' warned Stan, 'whatever you do, don't press that button!'